AND THE BAD APPLE

Want more Bibsy?

Bibsy Cross and the Bike-a-Thon

BIBSY CROSS

AND THE BAD APPLE

by Liz Garton Scanlon

illustrated by Dung Ho

Alfred A. Knopf

New York

THIS IS A BORZOI BOOK PUBLISHED BY ALFRED A. KNOPF

Visit us on the Web! rhcbooks.com

Educators and librarians, for a variety of teaching tools, visit us at RHTeachersLibrarians.com

Library of Congress Cataloging-in-Publication Data is available upon request.
ISBN 978-0-593-64441-6 (hardcover) — ISBN 978-0-593-64440-9 (pbk.) —
ISBN 978-0-593-64442-3 (lib. bdg.) — ISBN 978-0-593-64443-0 (ebook)

The text of this book is set in 13.5-point Bulmer MT Pro.
The illustrations were created using Photoshop.
Editors: Rotem Moscovich and Anne-Marie Varga
Designer: Monique Razzouk
Copy Editors: Colleen Fellingham and Artie Bennett
Managing Editor: Jake Eldred
Production Manager: Claribel Vasquez

MANUFACTURED IN CHINA
10 9 8 7 6 5 4 3 2 1
First Edition

For my friends at Longfellow Elementary,
a real constellation of light
–L.G.S.

For Tung, my whip-smart boy
–D.H.

I

In Bibsy's whole life,

she's only had one broken bone (wrist),

one set of stitches (chin),

and one mishap with scissors (her bangs).

She thinks that's plenty of excitement

for an eight-year-old

(although she *does* hope for braces someday).

Mostly, things are easy-peasy

and regular-pegular for Bibsy.

She is a whiz at counting backward

from a hundred and ten,

she can watch TV and finger-knit a scarf

at the same time (without looking down),

and she knows how to make a mean scrambled egg.

(Mean—that's what her dad calls it.

Bibsy just calls it yummy.)

Also, she hardly ever forgets to feed the cat

or brush her teeth or return her library books.

See? Regular-pegular!

2

Sometimes, when Bibsy feels wild,
she rides her bike with just one hand,
waving the other overhead like a flag.
She pedals especially fast then
because fast feels (oddly) sturdy,
and sturdy is really what she's aiming for.

Bibsy loves weekends and waving
and being just that teensiest bit wild.

But what she loves (loves, loves!)
most of all is school. Talk about sturdy.
School is as sturdy as a three-wheeled bike.

Bibsy loves the bell that begins the day,
and eating lunch from a tray,
and walking down the hall in big, snaky lines
(even when Josh steps on the heels
of her sneakers and turns them into flip-flops).

In kindergarten, Bibsy loved Ms. Range,
who helped them raise caterpillars
till they became butterflies,
and in first grade she loved Mr. Holmes,
who taught them how many pennies are in a dollar,
and then came Ms. Pike, who always
found time to read one more chapter,
no matter what. Bibsy maybe loved her
best of all.

Who Bibsy *doesn't* love
is this year's teacher—Mrs. Stumper.
Mrs. Stumper doesn't seem that keen
on Bibsy either.

Mrs. Stumper thinks Bibsy talks too much,
which isn't true. She's just a third grader
with a whole lot to say.

3

"So, that's it for today," says Mrs. Stumper, after explaining just the eensiest, teensiest bit about electricity. Mrs. Stumper only ever explains the eensiest, teensiest bits, even if some people want more more more.

Bibsy raises her hand.
Mrs. Stumper sighs.
Bibsy keeps her hand up.
"Yes, Bibsy?" says Mrs. Stumper.

(Bibsy considers this a victory,
since Mrs. Stumper called her Elizabeth
for the first two weeks of third grade,
even though Bibsy reminded her a hundred times
that she really feels most like a Bibsy.)

"I just wanted to say," says Bibsy,
"that there are these moving things
called currents, sort of like ocean currents,
only these ones are in electricity, and—"

"Is this a question, Bibsy?
This doesn't sound like a question," says Mrs. Stumper.

Mrs. Stumper is right—it is not a question.
Bibsy just wants to share.
That's what *she* calls it—sharing.
But Mrs. Stumper calls it "going on,"
as in, "You certainly do go on, Bibsy Cross."

4

Sometimes Mrs. Stumper feels
that Bibsy goes on a stone too far,
like when she explains static electricity and how to
use a balloon to make your hair stand on end,
and then again when she says, "Another important word
is 'voltage' because voltage is what *causes* currents."
Because who *wouldn't* want to know about voltage?!

Well, apparently Mrs. Stumper, that's who.
"Bibsy," she says, "I asked you three times

to please stop talking, and you just plain didn't.
I think that's a stone too far."

And then she turns toward
the great big corkboard apple tree,
bright with construction paper apples—
one for each kid, their names
in big black letters—

and she moves Bibsy's apple
from its high sweet spot in the green leaves
down to the bottom, sticking it
to the brown dirt at the base of the tree
with double-stick tape.

Personally, Bibsy thinks
that's a stone too far.

5

Each and every time Mrs. Stumper
walks to the corkboard
to drop Bibsy's apple to the ground
(which happens more often
than either of them likes),
Bibsy sucks in a quick bit of air
and rewinds her thoughts, wishing
she could go backward,
wishing Mrs. Stumper could see
that she is just regular-pegular,

wishing Mrs. Stumper liked her
the way she liked other kids,
the way she liked Mina, maybe
(even if she does have a lot to say!).

For some people, of course, it is even worse.
Some people (okay, mostly Marcus)
have an actual hole punched in their apple
nearly every week. (Sometimes more
than one hole.) A hole means a worm
has gotten to your apple. A hole means
it's rotten. A hole means
you've gone a stone too far
a bunch of times in the same day.

Marcus never seems to mind.
He usually just laughs,
which is what most people *like*
about Marcus. But it is what drives Mrs. Stumper
to distraction. That's what she says:
"You're driving me to absolute distraction, Marcus."

And that's when everyone else
(even Josh, who's also pretty distracting)
tries very hard not to get a hole punched
in their own apple. Maybe especially Bibsy.

Bibsy worries about her apple,
but she worries about Marcus's apple, too.
She sucks in a little breath of air for him,
even though he doesn't seem to mind
when Mrs. Stumper gets driven to distraction,
when she drops his apple, when she makes
a wormhole with the silver hole punch

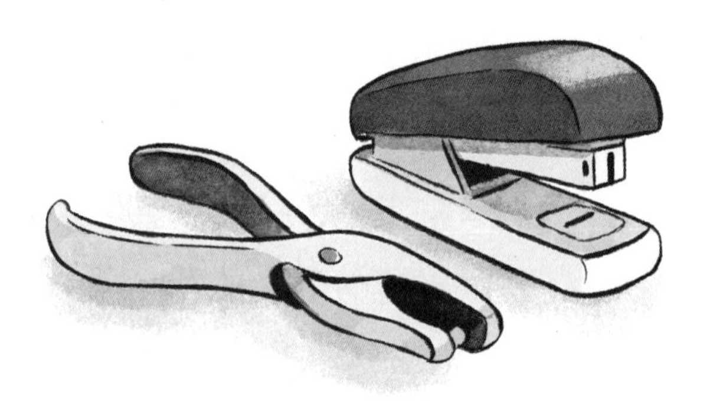

that sounds like a stapler. Bibsy sucks in a little breath of air for Marcus and his apple. She thinks, *Staplers are better than hole punches. They connect things.*

6

There is no actual going backward,
of course, but each morning Bibsy's apple
is rehung in the branches of the corkboard tree.
So is Marcus's. So are all the other
dropped-down apples from the day before.

When Mrs. Stumper rehangs them,
when she tucks them back up
among the bright green leaves—
Bibsy's and the other bruised and holey ones

right next to the ones like Mina's,

that never, ever even wobble—

Bibsy admires them all the same,

their round red sweetness,

their possibility and promise.

And each Friday, she takes her apple

from Mrs. Stumper in both hands,

like it is still something to be proud of,
never mind the days spent stuck in the dirt.

Bibsy brushes it off, as if
it were *real* dirt on a *real* apple,
as if she could polish away the week,
before taking it home, before sharing it
with her mom and dad.

7

At dinner, Bibsy and her mom and dad
go around the table and share their good
and not-so-good news—sweet-and-sours,
they call them. Sometimes Bibsy mentions
Mrs. You-Know-Who, but not often.
And sometimes she does go on,
but nobody ever says
it's a stone too far.

"So, my sour is that my tire went flat
on the way to school, and you know
what a hummer of a bummer it is
to have your sour come first thing
in the morning because of how
it can make your whole day
go that way . . . ?"

Bibsy pauses as her mom and dad
both make sourpuss puckers
to show that they *do* know,
they really, really do.

"So then I pushed my bike
instead of riding it—well,
Natia helped me, but still,
my backpack weighed
a hundred thousand pounds
and I was going so, so, so slowly
that I saw a chrysalis! Attached to a leaf!
Shaking, like it wanted to become
a butterfly right that minute!"

(Bibsy's parents are not surprised
by this story. If there is one true thing
about Bibsy, it is that her sours
almost always become sweet.)

"Oh gosh, Bibs," says her dad. "That's a beautiful . . ."

". . . turn of events," says her mom.

"You are our own personal butterfly," Dad says.

"You really are," says Mom, and Bibsy smiles and sighs and shakes a little—like a chrysalis. For once, she has nothing to say.

8

Bibsy's best friend Natia lives two doors down
on Arbor Street. Bibsy and Natia did
one hundred percent of everything together
until this year. This year is when Natia got Mr. Moon
and Bibsy, of course, got Mrs. Stumper.

Natia doesn't rub it in, but she doesn't have to.
The bulletin board outside Mr. Moon's class
is decorated like the night sky—
Mr. Moon and his Constellation of Light.

That's what he calls his class:
his Constellation of Light.

EVERYONE IN MR. MOON'S CLASS IS A STAR STUDENT
says the bright yellow lettering
running along the top of the bulletin board.

Bibsy looks at the stars—
Natia's and Cora's and Oliver's,
hung high and glittery and bright—
each time she walks down the third-grade hallway
toward Mrs. Stumper's room
and the great big corkboard apple tree.

She notices that Mr. Moon
never drops a single star
from the sky.

9

Here's the thing about
Bibsy and Natia.
They are almost
practically
nearly
identical
except for things
they can't help.

Like, Bibsy is forty-eight inches tall
and Natia is fifty-three inches tall,
so Natia's braids
brush the top of Bibsy's head
when they stand right next to each other,
which is pretty often.

And Natia has two sisters,
Nika and Camilla,
who are the itsiest, bitsiest bit
annoying, but mostly cute.
Bibsy has zero sisters
unless you count Natia
in an honorary way,
which, of course, Bibsy does.

Bibsy prefers pie and Natia prefers cake
and Bibsy prefers cats and Natia prefers dogs.
Which is weird. They really can't explain it.

Oh, and maybe the most important thing,
at least as far as someone like
Mrs. Stumper is concerned?

Natia never goes a stone too far.

10

“Y’know how they split us up this year?” says Natia.
She and Bibsy pedal home, side by side.

“Yep. Split like atoms,” Bibsy says,
shaking her helmeted head.

“These are our darkest days!” says Natia.

“Yep,” says Bibsy, “the darkest.”

"Well, good news," says Natia.
"Brighter days ahead!"

Bibsy perks up. She senses a sour turning sweet
right before her very eyes.

The girls stop at the light to walk their bikes
across the street, just like they're supposed to,
even though all the other kids on the planet
pedal wildly past, as if rules were as slippery as ice.

"Okay, I'm ready," says Bibsy, once they're safely
on the other side. "Tell me about brighter days."

"Mr. Moon says science fair partners
don't have to be in the same class," says Natia.
"Which means . . ."

Bibsy knows what this means!

STOP
BUS

Natia doesn't even need to finish—
Bibsy one hundred percent knows
exactly what this means.

She pedals faster,
lifts one hand off her handlebar,
and whoops and waves.

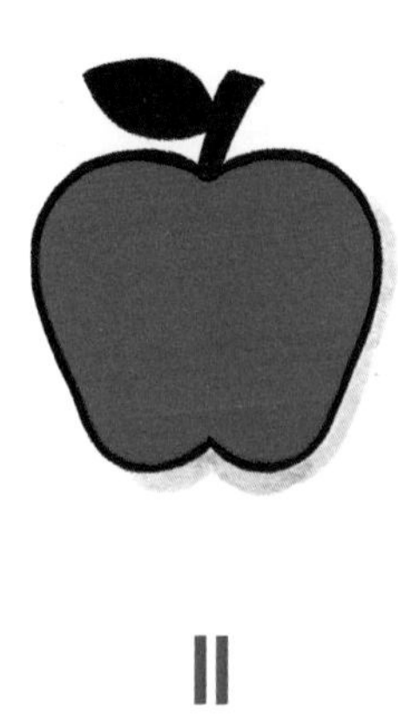

11

The next day, Mrs. Stumper explains
just the eensiest, teensiest bit
about science fair. Of course.

"Pick an idea. A *manageable* idea.
Do research, using reliable sources.
Multiple reliable sources.
Undertake the experiment

and report your findings.
Your *proven* findings."

Mina nods along,
like she already knows
everything there is to know
about science fair.

Bibsy raises her hand.
Mrs. Stumper sighs.
Bibsy keeps her hand up.
"Yes, Bibsy," says Mrs. Stumper.

"Well," says Bibsy, "the important thing is—"
"Is this a question, Bibsy? This doesn't sound
like a question," says Mrs. Stumper.

"Not exactly, but I just wanted to say

we should brainstorm, right?" Bibsy is proud she turned that suggestion into a question after all.

"Like, not everybody should just put pennies in lemon juice or whatever," she adds.

"Hey!" says Mina.

(Mina's second-grade
science fair experiment had to do
with pennies and lemon juice.)

"No offense, Mina," says Bibsy.

"Bibsy Cross, you do go on," says Mrs. Stumper.
Bibsy raises her hand again.
"Bibsy?" Mrs. Stumper says,
even though she looks like she'd rather not.

"I just meant that we should . . .
be creative," says Bibsy.
Everyone likes the sound of that. Even Mina.
"Also? I wanted to share that we can partner
with kids from Mr. Moon's class!
Right, Mrs. Stumper?" says Bibsy.

Mrs. Stumper sighs again, but she says,
"Right, Bibsy. That's absolutely right."

Bibsy closes her eyes for a moment,
breathing in Mrs. Stumper's actual approval
and then picturing her partner, worlds away,
floating in Mr. Moon's Constellation of Light.

12

“Let’s do something really cool,” says Bibsy.

“And really advanced,” says Natia.

“Yes,” says Bibsy. “Actual, grown-up science.”

Bibsy and Natia lie on their backs
in the grass in Bibsy’s backyard,
their legs propped up against the trunk
of the old oak tree, feet pointing
toward the sky.

"Not something with Play-Doh
or pennies or whatever," says Natia.
"Exactly what I'm saying!"
Bibsy's feet push excitedly
up, up, up toward the sky.

"Maybe like a catapult . . ."
"Or something with electricity . . ."
"Or bacteria . . ."
"Or gravity . . ."
"Ooooooh, gravity!"

All four of the girls' feet drop down
to Earth then, with a satisfying *thud*
(. . . thud, thud, thud).

"It's decided," says Bibsy.
"Yep," says Natia.
"And it's gonna be good," says Bibsy.
"So good," says Natia.

13

"As you all know, today's the day
your proposals are due."

Mrs. Stumper stands at the whiteboard
and points to the word "Proposal"
one, two, three times—
like it's a spelling word instead of
an activity, like it's something
to memorize and move on from
instead of the beginning

of the best science fair project
on the planet.

Bibsy raises her hand.
Mrs. Stumper sighs.
Bibsy keeps her hand up.
"Really, Bibsy?" says Mrs. Stumper.

"Yes, Mrs. Stumper," says Bibsy.
Mrs. Stumper sighs.
Bibsy stands.

"So, our proposal? Mine and Natia's?"
She says it like that, with question marks
at the end, because Mrs. Stumper
likes questions. Usually.

"Have a seat, Bibsy," says Mrs. Stumper.

"But what I was saying," says Bibsy,
and even as the words form in her mouth,
even as she hears herself say,
"I think we should go around the room
and share. Because our proposal,
mine and Natia's? Is totally wow!
Some might say sensational, and . . ."

Even as her heart races and her cheeks flush,
even as she hears her words tumble out,
one after the other, she knows she's gone
a stone too far.

14

The thing about sweet-and-sours
is that there are always several
to choose from, each and every day,
so Bibsy never actually has to share
that her apple was plucked from
its branch and dropped down
to the dirt below.

"I stubbed my toe so hard,
the school shook," Bibsy says.

Or "I got chosen fifteenth in gym, even though
I'm technically faster than Kimmy McSoo,
which technically makes it a sweet
because Kimmy is pretty fast."
Or "Marcus spilled his milk at lunch,
which I guess is technically Marcus's sour,
except he spilled it on me!"

Never does she ever mention her apple.

Her mom says the printer at work ran out of ink,
and her dad says he bought a huge bag
of the wrong kind of cat food—and the cat agrees.

It goes on like this, so nobody knows
that the worst, hardest, most bruising
sour of all is Bibsy's apple double-stick-taped
to the dirt at the very bottom
of the corkboard tree right this very minute.

Nobody knows but Bibsy.

15

Materials:

string

paper clips

a cardboard box

magnets

"I wish we didn't have to list the materials . . . ," says Bibsy.

". . . because it kind of gives away
the secret behind the science," says Natia.

Natia and Bibsy often finish
each other's sentences.
They aren't even surprised
when it happens.

"If it were up to me," says Bibsy,
"I'd write 'magnets' in invisible ink."

"Or magnetic ink," says Natia,
which is the funniest thing ever,
even if it doesn't exist.

16

In Mr. Moon's class, when you complete
a step for your science fair project,
you get a gold star.

Your proposal? A gold star.
Research notes? A gold star.
Question, hypothesis, prediction? Gold stars.
The actual experiment? Another proud, shiny star
stuck to the name chart near the cubbies
at the back of the room.

Bibsy knows this because
she gets extra-special permission
to go to Mr. Moon's room
to work with Natia during science.

"Be on your absolute best behavior,"
says Mrs. Stumper as Bibsy skips
out the door. "Make me proud."

The only disappointing thing, thinks Bibsy,
is not having her own name
written in silver script next to Natia's
on Mr. Moon's star chart.

17

One of the great things about science
is how you make discoveries along the way.
Like, for example, how Bibsy and Natia
planned to design a space scene,
which made sense because everyone
thinks of space when they think of gravity,
and also because of Mr. Moon
and his Constellation of Light.

But then, smack in the middle
of the research process (gold star!),
Bibsy discovers Isaac Newton.

"Isaac Newton was one of the first
scientists to sort of understand
gravity," says Bibsy, "because, get this,
he saw . . ."

Bibsy pauses to build suspense.

Natia does a drumroll
with her fingers on the table.

". . . because he saw an *apple* fall from a tree!"
"An apple? No way!"
"Yes! YES WAY!"
"How perfect for your apple-dropping teacher!"

Yes! Bibsy can hardly believe it herself.

Gravity Apples!

Mrs. Stumper won't be able to resist.

She'll love their project!

She might even grow to love Bibsy

the itsiest, bitsiest bit.

"So, you're thinking . . ."

". . . we'll make an apple orchard . . ."

“. . . and a little paper doll of Isaac Newton . . .”

“. . . inside our cardboard box!”

“Exactly,” say Bibsy and Natia

at the exact same time.

“Jinx blinks,” they say

at the same time, too.

18

Question:
Can a magnetic force
be stronger and mightier
than the pull of gravity?

Hypothesis:
Gravity is a force that attracts
objects toward one another
(like an apple falling to the ground
like it's being pulled), but magnetism

is its own force
that can resist gravity.

Prediction:
If we add a powerful magnetic field
to an apple orchard, the fallen apples
will defy gravity and rise back up
to the branches. Like magic,
only realer than that.

19

Most days during science,
Bibsy and Natia work side by side
in Mr. Moon's room,
trying out different magnets
paired with different paper clips,
learning more about Isaac Newton
and his apple tree, sketching
the lush, leafy backdrop
of their diorama.

Natia's braids brush Bibsy's
bowed head as the girls work.
It feels right.
They are happy.

Soon, Bibsy feels herself
automatically turn toward
Mr. Moon's room each morning,
as if that's where she really belongs.

"Look," says Mr. Moon on Friday
when Bibsy arrives yet again,
all regular-pegular, no big deal,
"it's our honorary star!"

Bibsy beams.

20

20

When you're biking home alone
because your very best friend
from two doors down is at the dentist,
and your second, third, and fourth best friends
(no offense, Mina) take the bus
or live in the other direction,
and you've got a sensational
cardboard box (otherwise known as
a scientific diorama)

in your bike basket
and it starts to rain?

That is a serious sour.
A mucky, droopy, blurry,
soggy sour. It's hard
to find any sweetness in it,
even for Bibsy.

“Well,” says Bibsy’s mom,
“I guess wet cardboard is one way
to demonstrate the effects
of gravity.”

“Good one,” says Bibsy,
but she is not a fan
of wet cardboard
or of having to start over.

Dad leans across his dinner plate
and rubs Bibsy’s back.
“Sorry, Bibs,” he says.
Which is, in its own way, a sweet.

21

"So, moving on," says Mrs. Stumper,
pointing yet again to her whiteboard.
"You all should be basically done by now.
I've given you more than enough time. . . ."

Bibsy raises her hand.
Mrs. Stumper sighs.
Bibsy keeps her hand up.
"Yes, Bibsy?" says Mrs. Stumper.

"The thing is," says Bibsy,
and she takes a deep breath,
ready to explain the rain
and the ruined cardboard,
ready to explain everything
the way she had with Natia,
only she is hoping to do it without tears
this time. (She didn't mind
crying in front of Natia.)

"The thing is . . . ," Bibsy says again,
so sad, so sorry, and so willing to start
from scratch, to get it right.

Mrs. Stumper sighs and shakes her head,
but that doesn't stop Bibsy.

"It's just that we were so close
and our work was so good. I mean,

I really think you're gonna love it, Mrs. Stumper!
It's all about apples? I mean, at least sort of,
but also gravity? And Isaac Newton—
do you know Isaac Newton? But then the rain . . .
this is such a shocking truth . . . the rain ruined . . .
everything, or almost everything?
And now we need . . ."

Bibsy made as many of her statements
into questions as she could,
but they just kept coming,
faster and faster, blurring together
like the inky trunk and branches
in the ruined diorama,
question after question after question,
like rain that couldn't resist the fall.

"That will do, Bibsy Cross," says Mrs. Stumper,
but Bibsy has more to say, and she hears herself

say, "But no, wait," and "I'm so, so serious,"
and even "Listen to me, Mrs. Stumper!"

She hears herself explaining
and double-explaining,
asking—begging, really—
to go to Mr. Moon's room
just one last time.

"It'll be worth it, Mrs. Stumper,"
says Bibsy. "You'll see."

But Mrs. Stumper *doesn't* see,
because she's turned her back
on Bibsy, she's dropping Bibsy's apple
to the ground, and Bibsy hears
her own words hitting the floor
in big, fat drops of "No, no, no, no, no."

Everyone stares at her then—
Mina and Marcus and Kimmy and Josh
and, well, everyone. Everyone
stares at her and thinks, *There goes Bibsy.*
Bibsy's doing it again.

22

When you go a stone too far
more than once in the same day
(yes, like Marcus), your apple
doesn't just drop to the dirt.
That's bad enough.

But when Mrs. Stumper
has really, truly had it
(she says that sometimes—
"Enough," she says.

“I have really, truly had it with all this nonsense!”), she punches a hole in your apple with her silver hole punch, which sounds like a stapler but isn’t.

This has never, ever happened to Bibsy before. Bibsy’s apple drops on a regular basis, but it is always red and round and whole, and it’s always lifted back up

red and round and whole each morning
and sent home each Friday
bright and unbattered.

Until this week. Until today.

23

A bad apple is not the same
as a broken wrist.
It's not the same as cracking
your chin open
on the side of the swimming pool.
It's not a real wound,
but it feels like one.

It's as if Bibsy has something stuck
in her throat—that's how it feels.

And it's only Wednesday.

Bibsy doesn't know
how she will stand
seeing her apple nestled
back among the leaves
tomorrow, hole and all.
She doesn't know
how she will stand
the slowness of every hour
from now until Friday,
and she doesn't know

how she will possibly stand
taking the apple from Mrs. Stumper
with both hands, and bringing it home
to her mom and dad.

At dinner, Bibsy says she doesn't have a sour.
"Oh! Well, that's a good day!" says her mom.
"Or a sweet," says Bibsy.
"Oh," says her dad. "Maybe not so good."

They make sourpuss puckers then.

"I mean, I guess I just don't feel well," says Bibsy,

and she realizes that's the honest truth.

She doesn't. It *is* like a real wound after all.

24

“Where were you yesterday?” asks Natia
as she rolls to a stop in front of Bibsy’s house.
“I looked for you after school. . . .”

Natia stops talking.

Bibsy is there, with her bike and her backpack,
but it’s also almost like she’s not there.

“Bibsy? Are you . . . okay?
I thought we were going to
start redoing our diorama?”
She says it in a not-mad way
because she’s Natia, because
she’s already forgiven
both Bibsy and the rain.

But this isn’t about that.
This is worse. Much worse.
Bibsy opens her mouth, wanting
to tell Natia about the bad apple,
but she finds she can’t make words at all.
So she pushes her bike down the driveway,
and they pedal toward school, walk their bikes
across the crosswalk, and lock them up together, quietly.

Then they stand for a second outside Mr. Moon’s room,
looking at the stars on his corkboard

and looking at each other.

They say, "Okay, well . . ."

And then they say, "Jinx blinks"

and smile.

25

Mrs. Stumper acts
like it's a plain old regular-pegular
Think Hard Thursday.
Like Mina should go right ahead
with taking attendance,
and Josh should change the calendar,
and Kimmy should collect all the library books.

Like everyone should be ready
for music and lunch and spelling.

CALENDAR
March

Like Bibsy's diorama should be dry
and done. Like her apple, back up
among the branches, doesn't have
a gaping hole that everyone can see.

When Mrs. Stumper gives her lesson,
Bibsy does not raise her hand.
She does not have questions. She does not
have the eensiest, teensiest
thought to share.

Mrs. Stumper even pauses a time or two,
looks at Bibsy, and waits.
But she does not go on at all,
much less a stone too far.

26

When Bibsy meets Natia in the lunch line,
she's still worried and sad and mad.
There's still some sort of feeling that's stuck
in her throat. But she's also just plain tired
of being quiet. So she goes ahead and says it:
"Natia, I have to share a shocking truth.
Mrs. Stumper punched a hole in my apple."

Natia stops sliding her tray along the cafeteria counter
and looks at Bibsy.

“That,” says Natia, “is really rotten.”

Which is funny, right? A rotten apple?
Bibsy doesn’t exactly laugh, but she sure is grateful.

The girls get their tacos and their fruit cups
and their milk, and they sit at the third table back
on the left side, smack in the middle of a sunbeam,
so their lunches actually sparkle.

"Should we work at your house or my house this afternoon?" Bibsy asks.

"Don't worry about it," says Natia. "We can finish this weekend. We're fast, and it's just . . . science fair."

"Just science fair?" says Bibsy.
"We've got the best project on the planet!
Or we will. Once we redo it."

"But your apple!" says Natia.

Science fair does not care about a hole in Bibsy's apple. Even Bibsy knows that.

"I have to pick myself up and brush myself off," she says. "I have to defy gravity."

27

Five things on a Friday:

Bibsy and Natia *did* defy gravity, together.
Their diorama is practically better than ever already.

When Mina calls attendance,
Marcus says, “Thank goobers it’s Friday!”
instead of “Here,” and the whole class laughs.

Lunch is fish sticks with tartar sauce.

Kimmy hands out birthday party invitations
to everyone in the whole class, including Bibsy.

And at the end of the day, as they walk
out of the room, one by one by one,
Mrs. Stumper hands them each their apple.

Bibsy looks at the hole in hers—
perfectly centered, perfectly round,
and perfectly achy.
She sucks in a little air then,
and tries to rewind time.

28

The minutes between after school
and dinner move in slow motion for Bibsy,
like honey coming out of a little plastic bear,
honey hanging thick and heavy over waiting toast.

Except that's not quite right,
because honey
is most definitely a sweet.

This? Tonight? Handing over
her bad apple? A slow-motion sour.

"I don't want to brag," says Dad,
"but I think you'll find this pasta
to be beyond compare."

Dad often says his meals are
"beyond compare," and how would Bibsy know,
when she has nothing to compare them *to*?

"So. Friday. Whew, what a week," says Mom.
"Let's go around . . ."

Bibsy gets it. This is how they do things.
They take turns. They take their time.
They laugh and tease and talk about pasta
and Fridays and all things regular-pegular.

But tonight is most definitely not
regular-pegular, and Bibsy can't stand it,
not for one more minute.

"I can't stand it," she says,
"not for one more minute!"

"What?" says Mom.
"You can't stand what?" says Dad.
"My apple," says Bibsy. "*This* apple."

And she puts it in the middle of the table,
between them. Then, as if they can't see
for themselves, she says, "It's got a hole in it.
Mrs. Stumper punched a hole in my apple."

And as her mom and dad look
back and forth, at the bad apple
and then at Bibsy and at each other,

Bibsy does what she's been waiting to do since Wednesday:

She starts to cry.

29

Bibsy's mom and dad each reach
for one of her hands and give her
a little squeeze.
Bibsy squeezes back.

Her mom reminds her
that this is not a real apple
or a real wormhole.
"It's just paper," she says.
"It's just an idea."

"Sort of a bad idea," says Bibsy.
Her mom makes a sourpuss pucker
to show she agrees.

Her dad reminds her
that *she's* not an apple either.
She's a living, breathing third grader
with a human head and heart
that matter a whole lot more
than a construction paper idea.

"I do go on, though," says Bibsy.
Bibsy's mom and dad shrug.
"Sometimes I go on
a stone too far," she adds.

"Oh, Bibs," says her dad,
"you just have . . ."

". . . a lot to say," says her mom.

(Bibsy's mom and dad finish
each other's sentences,
just like Bibsy and Natia do.)

Bibsy wipes her eyes.
"You don't think I'm rotten?" she asks.

"Honey!" says Mom. "Most certainly not!
You are the sweetest!"
Bibsy feels her fingers unclench.

"Yep, you're sweet as pie," says Dad.
Bibsy feels her heartbeats settle.

"Speaking of which . . . ," says Dad,
and he's off to the kitchen
to rustle up dessert.

"Yum," says Bibsy. And she smiles.

30

It's Sunday, the day before Monday,
and it's time for finishing touches.
In houses up this street and down that one,
kids type up purpose statements
and procedures, they measure beanstalks
and balance scales. They draw conclusions.

They use bright purple glue sticks
to arrange graphs and tables and photos
on their trifold presentation boards.

And a certain pair of starry-eyed pals
on Arbor Street balance extra magnets
atop their box because they do not intend
to let their apples give in to gravity,
no matter how strong
a force it may be.

31

Bibsy and Natia agree to walk
their science fair project to school
Monday morning. No bike baskets,
no big risks, no unnecessary drama.

When they arrive, safe and sound,
they go straight to the gymnasium,
straight to their assigned spot,
with board and box, apples and attitude.

HOW DO YOU LIKE THEM APPLES?
BIBSY and NATIA
DEFY
ISAAC NEWTON'S GRAVITY
ABOUT Sir Isaac Newton
ABOUT Gravity
ABOUT Magnetism
Question
Procedures
Resources
Hypothesis
Materials
Conclusion

32

When you get a hole
punched in your apple,
a responsible adult
is required to sign it.

Bibsy wonders
if Marcus's responsible adults
ever get tired of that requirement.

After setting up for science fair,
and hanging her backpack in her cubby,
Bibsy marches up to Mrs. Stumper
and hands over her signed apple.

Then she raises her hand.
Mrs. Stumper doesn't sigh.
She actually sort of laughs,
the eensiest, teensiest bit.

"Bibsy," she says,
"it's just you and me here.
No need to raise your hand."

Bibsy lowers her hand and says,
"I know I do go on sometimes, Mrs. Stumper,
and I'm sorry. But I want you to know
I'm not a bad apple. I'm just regular-pegular!"

Mrs. Stumper listens and shakes her head,
and then, like a star showing up
just as the sun goes down,
she smiles softly.

"I know, Bibsy. I know you are.
Well, maybe not *quite* regular-pegular. . . ."

"Maybe not quite," agrees Bibsy.
Then she takes a big, brave breath.
"But even not-quite-regular-pegulars
have feelings, and the hole you punched
in this apple hurt mine."

Mrs. Stumper stops smiling. "Oh!" she says.

"Hole punches hurt Marcus's feelings, too,"
says Bibsy, even though she's not
one hundred percent sure that's true.

"Well, that was not my intention.
Thank you for sharing, Bibsy."

"You're welcome," says Bibsy.
"I just have so much . . ."

". . . to say," says Mrs. Stumper, nodding.

Then she points in the direction of Bibsy's desk,
and Bibsy takes the hint. She's sitting down
and getting out her pencil and paper before she realizes
that Mrs. Stumper finished her sentence.

33

The judges—"esteemed community members,"
as Mr. Moon called them in his opening remarks—
walk slowly around the gymnasium, stopping
to learn a little bit about each project.
When they get to Bibsy and Natia,
they nod, and one of them says,
"Well, what have we here?"

Natia and Bibsy have rehearsed
the whole thing. The way they're going to pretend

SCIENCE FAIR
POPCORN
LEMON BATTERY
THE LIFE CYCLE OF A BUTTERFLY
SOLAR SYSTEM
GROW A RAINBOW
THE EXPLOSIVE TRUTH

like their presentation is all about gravity.
The way they're going to introduce Isaac Newton
and his discovery and the fact that these apples
(otherwise known as decorated paper clips)
fell straight down from the branches above,
just barely missing his head.
They've even rehearsed the awe they'll express.

Then—and this is where it gets fun—
Bibsy says, "But a law is just an idea.
And ideas aren't always perfect. Or right."

"Sometimes other ideas come along,"
says Natia, "that might present a challenge!"

"They might be even stronger than
the original idea!" says Bibsy, slipping
three little magnets out of her pocket
and pressing them against the back of the box
(otherwise known as the apple orchard).

“Like magnetism!” says Natia, popping both hands out in a little unrehearsed jazz-ma-tazz situation.

And then, to the amazement of all three judges (and to Isaac Newton, too, it looks like), the apples

rise up from the bottom of the box
and float, wavering a bit, like hopes or wishes,
before settling, bright and unbattered,
back into the branches,
where they belong.

34

After lunch, everyone gets to
walk around the whole gymnasium
and look at the volcanoes and the trebuchets
and—yes—the pennies in lemon juice.

Natia thinks the funniest and most amazing display
is the video of Cora and Oliver training a cat
to come to dinner by ringing a bike bell.

Bibsy likes Marcus and Josh's presentation
on how stitches work,
even if their (kind of gruesome) real-life photos
go a stone too far.

Honestly, they're all really good. Even Mina's!
Everyone has a ribbon on their board—
blue, red, or white—plus notes and compliments
from the judges and teachers and other students.

When Bibsy and Natia circle all the way back around
to their apple orchard, there's a blue ribbon
stuck to the side of their box
and, right in the middle of the sheet
of congratulations and high fives,
a note from Mrs. Stumper that reads,
"Isaac Newton and I agree—
a very 'uplifting' presentation!"

Which was both nice *and* funny!

Bibsy is . . . well . . . stunned speechless.

So much so that it takes a minute

for her to notice their tiny diorama apples,

still hanging like magic from their branches,

made even brighter and bolder and luckier

by the addition of not one but two

of Mr. Moon's gold stars.

"A real constellation of light," says Bibsy,
suddenly feeling pretty stellar
and not regular-pegular *at all.*

Buckle up and join Bibsy as she bikes for books!

Read on for a sneak peek.

Published by Alfred A. Knopf, an imprint of Random House Children's Books,
a division of Penguin Random House LLC, New York.

I

Bibsy is really, mostly,
a regular-pegular ol' kid,
with just a little extra . . . everything.

She is the kind of person
who means what she says.
Who goes big or goes home.
Who nearly hugs the stuffing
straight out of her cat.

She loves what she loves
(and that includes her best friend, Natia,
and reading out loud in funny voices
and finger-knitting foot-long scarves
and signing up for things).

Also, dessert.
Bibsy is a big fan of dessert.

Then there's her bike. Bibsy loves her bike
beyond measure. She rides every day,
hot or cold, rain or shine.

Sometimes she pretends
it's a horse
or a chariot
or a convertible.

Sometimes she pedals like a kitchen mixer,

waving one hand overhead and letting
the trees and houses and mailboxes race by
like a blurry movie.

Sometimes she pretends her bike is the wind.
Bibsy maybe loves that most of all.